ONLY YOU CAN SAVE Christmas!

A Help-the-Elf Adventure

New York Times bestselling author
Adam Wallace

pictures by
Garth Bruner

sourcebooks
jabberwocky

Everything was going fine until
just a couple of minutes ago.

I made my list...

OH NO!
This *must* be a list of things Santa wants to give to Mrs. Claus.

But he's been so busy getting ready for everyone else, he hasn't had any time for himself!

THE TWELVE DAYS OF CHRISTMAS

My true love gave to me . . .

1 partridge in a pear tree

2 turtle doves

3 French hens

4 calling birds

5 gold rings

6 geese a-laying

7 swans a-swimming

8 maids a-milking

9 ladies dancing

10 lords a-leaping

11 pipers piping

12 drummers drumming

For mom and dad, who forever encourage my antics.
—GB

Published by Sourcebooks, Inc.
P.O. Box 4410, Naperville, Illinois 60567-4410
(630) 961-3900
Fax: (630) 961-2168
sourcebooks.com

Library of Congress Cataloging-in-Publication Data is on file with the publisher.

Source of Production: Leo Paper, Heshan City, Guangdong Province, China
Date of Production: June 2017
Run Number: 5009685

Printed and bound in China.
LEO 10 9 8 7 6 5 4 3 2 1

How about a turtle?